COMING OF AGE 2: THE DAY OF SELF PLEASURE

CLOVER'S FANTASY ADVENTURES
BOOK 14

VICTORIA RUSH

VOLUME 14

CLOVER'S FANTASY ADVENTURES -
BOOK 14

AUTHOR'S NOTE

All characters in this work of fiction are at least eighteen years of age.

COPYRIGHT

For the uninhibited...

1

———

After the three friends watched the sexy girl fucking the improvised rocking horse on the stage, they returned to their cabin, more stimulated and inspired than ever.

"Holy shit," Clover gushed, her pussy still throbbing and the insides of her thighs tingling from the dried streams of lubrication. "We have *got* to get ourselves one of those things. I've never seen that kind of fucking machine before!"

"It was pretty hot," Tara nodded, her own pussy still aching from the thrusting action of her hands in and out of her hole.

"It was fun to watch a *girl* using it," Jessop chuckled. "But it wouldn't work so well for me."

"I dunno," Clover grinned. "It wouldn't be so difficult for you to make a few adjustments to the mechanism to create an artificial *pussy* instead of a hard dildo..."

"Maybe so," Jessop said. "But I've got something else in mind for my next performance. Something I'm sure none of these natives have even *dreamed* of before–"

"Are you going to give us a little peek before you go

public with the rest of the group?" Tara said, pinching her eyebrows together in curiosity.

"It's not the sort of thing that's easily shared with others," Jessop said. "It's better that I save it for the safety of the sheltered stage."

"Ooo," Clover teased. "So cryptic and mysterious, all of a sudden. It's not like you to be so tight-lipped about your sexual preferences."

"I'll be happy to unseal them if you need me to satisfy certain *other* cravings," he smiled, staring at the girls' glistening vulvas. "It's only my throbbing *cock* that I need to save for tomorrow."

"Hmm," Clover said, peering at her other friend. "What do you say, Tara? Do you want to have a late-night quickie before we turn in for the night?"

"I was kind of looking forward to riding Jessop's thumper after watching that native girl get off on the horse's dick, but a pair of moist lips might do the job just as well," Tara nodded.

"How about *two* pairs?" Clover grinned. "I'm tired of watching solo performances. As far as I'm concerned, the more live bodies we can play with at the same time, the better."

"Do you want me to be on the bottom this time?" Tara said, jumping onto the bed and spreading her legs wide apart as she rolled over onto her back.

"Works for me," Clover nodded, crawling overtop of Tara and swinging her body around until her dripping pussy levitated over her head while Jessop lay down between Tara's legs and planted his face in her pussy.

"Mmm," Tara purred as Clover lowered her steamy crotch over her face and licked her nipples while Jessop ate her cunt. "This is much better than a carved piece of wood..."

The following day, Jessop spent another large part of the afternoon foraging alone in the forest while the two girls worked together in the fields, then everyone assembled for a large communal feast in the amphitheater before preparing for the evening's next performance.

"Are you ready for the big show tonight?" Gisella asked Jessop, noticing his tool already swelling in anticipation of giving his first public demonstration.

"I think so," he said, winking at his friends. "But mine is a little more complicated than some of the others–"

"He's certainly spent enough time sneaking around the woods preparing for it," Tara chuckled. "We're just as excited as the rest of the tribe to see what he unveils."

"It better be good," Clover huffed. "Because you've spent enough time raising our expectations..."

"I hope to be raising a lot more than everyone's *expectations* this evening," he nodded.

A couple of hours later, as the candles around the stage were illuminated and the drummer began his beat signaling the tribe to take their seats in the big amphitheater, Jessop gathered his equipment and walked slowly toward the rear of the stage. His friends squinted into the darkening gloom, noticing him carrying a box-sized object in his right hand and a small wooden bucket in the other.

"What in God's name is he planning *this* time?" Tara said, shaking her head in curiosity.

"I have no idea," Clover said. "But if his performance will come close to matching the amount of time he's taken to prepare for the demonstration, it should be pretty interesting."

Jessop slowly ascended the stairs at the back of the platform, then he walked out to the center of the flickering stage, placing the large box and the smaller bucket next to him on the dais. The trio on the front row of the theater could hear a strange noise emanating from the box, and they turned to face one another with a puzzled expression.

"Is that what I think it is?" Tara said to Clover.

"If you mean a *bee colony*, then I think so," Tara nodded.

"What the hell is he going to do with that?" Clover said, widening her eyes. "It doesn't sound very erotic to me..."

"Maybe he's going to put them to work in a *different* kind of way," the old lady sitting next to them said as she watched Jessop reach down to lift up the small bucket.

He raised it over the top of his swelling instrument, then he tilted the bucket over the front of his bare mound, pouring a thick, yellow-colored liquid over his cock and balls.

"Is that...*honey*?" Tara said, shaking her head in disbelief.

"It certainly looks like it," the old lady said.

"Whatever is he planning to do with that?" Clover gasped.

"I'm not entirely sure," Gisella said, cocking her head to one side as she listened to the bees trapped inside the box buzzing more excitedly.

"Maybe he's going to use it as some kind of lubricant," Tara said, noticing Jessop's prick starting to rise and expand as it slowly rose over his belly.

"But it's *sticky*, not exactly slippery," Clover said. "That's the *last* thing I'd want to put on my private parts."

"On the other hand," Gisella smiled, watching Jessop sit down on the stage and pull the buzzing box closer to him.

"It *is* very tasty and nutritious. Perhaps he's not planning on touching himself at all."

The two girls' eyes suddenly flung open, and they turned their heads to gape at Gisella in shock.

"You don't think he's planning to let the bees *lick* it off his cock?" Clover said.

"Why not?" the old lady grinned. "Bees don't just make honey, they also eat it during the winter months when they're deprived of flower nectar."

"So *that's* what he's been doing these past few days alone in the forest," Tara nodded. "He's been trapping the bees and keeping them from their food sources..."

"And testing if they'll eat the honey off his own *skin*," Clover said.

"Let's hope they don't take out their anger from being trapped all alone by stinging his dick once he sets them free," Tara laughed.

Jessop lowered his upper body down onto the soft animal skins lining the platform, then he carefully raised a latch on top of the box and lifted the lid with one finger. The trapped bees swarmed out of the top and beelined directly toward his bobbing erection, coating it instantly in a thick blanket of buzzing and moving insects. Jessop moaned softly, then he dropped his arms off to the side and closed his eyes while the swarm of bees gorged on the sweet honey, covering his entire instrument and his tightening balls in a carpet of flapping insects.

"He seems to be enjoying the feeding frenzy," Clover said, staring at Jessop with eyes as wide as saucers.

"I'll say," Tara nodded. "Judging by how his erection is bouncing around from all the attention, I'd say he's finding it very stimulating."

"That's one hell of a unique *vibrator*, that's for sure,"

Clover chuckled, hardly aware that she'd been dripping like a faucet out of her pussy the whole time she was watching Jessop on the stage.

"A *what*?" Gisella said, peering at Clover with a wrinkled forehead.

"It's a kind of automated sex toy back where I come from," Clover nodded. "But I've never seen one quite like *that* before."

"Well, judging by the amount of noise he's making and his body language," Tara chuckled. "I'd say he's certainly enjoying the stimulation of his home-made sex toy."

The girls stared at Jessop squirming on the stage while his groaning began to escalate in pitch and his buttocks slowly rose over the surface of the platform as the honey dribbled between his legs and the crack of his ass, with the swirling blanket of bees swarming over his entire perineum.

"That's fucking *brilliant*," Clover said, circling her clit faster while she watched Jessop having the time of his life as the rest of the crowd stimulated themselves simultaneously. "He's using the honey to direct the bees' buzzing over his entire erogenous zone."

"I guess that explains why he came back from the forest with so many welts on his lower body," Tara laughed.

"I don't think they're leaving quite as many welts this time," Clover said, watching Jessop's face twisting into a delighted state of rapture while he tensed his muscles and arched his body upward with his swarming cock raised higher in the air.

Suddenly, he grunted out loud, then ten thick streams of white fluid shot up in the air in powerful pulses while the bees flew around his shaking body, lapping up the sticky liquid as it fell onto his chest and quivering legs.

"Fuck me," Tara groaned, clasping her thighs tightly

around her hands, deeply embedded in her pussy. "That was the weirdest and most erotic performance I've ever seen."

"It was pretty original," Clover nodded, shaking in kind while her own juices streamed down the crack of her ass like a waterfall.

"I'll say," Gisella said, holding two fingers deep inside her dripping cavern as she trembled silently on the step beside them. "I'd have to say he's the leading contender for top male performer of the month. If you play your cards right, one of you girls might have the chance to hook up with him publicly after you demonstrate your own version of auto-stimulation."

"We've got something unique planned," Tara said, winking toward Clover. "Do you think you can squeeze us into the schedule before the next full moon?"

"There's still almost two weeks left before it completes its cycle," the old lady nodded, peering up at the gleaming crescent in the night sky. "I'm pretty sure we can work at least *one* of you in."

2

———

After Jessop's unusual but intoxicating performance on the big amphitheater stage, the three friends returned to their cabin, more energized than ever.

"That was *insane*, Jess!" Clover said, poking him excitedly in the ribs and staring at his shrunken cock to make sure he wasn't covering in stings. "What were you thinking, letting a swarm of bees loose on your dick?"

"I was thinking how good it felt to have a hundred of them buzzing and flapping their wings over me at the same time," Jessop chuckled.

"Weren't you worried that some of them might sting you?" Tara said.

"I tested it pretty carefully out in the woods beforehand–"

"On your *dick*?" Clover said, arching a brow.

"Not exactly," Jessop said. "But they seemed pretty tame when I placed the honey on other parts of my body..."

"What did it feel like exactly?" Tara said, pinching his organ softly to make sure it wasn't covered in welts.

"It's hard to describe," Jessop said. "Kind of like a thousand insects sucking my cock from every possible angle."

"That was pretty ingenious," Clover laughed. "Wherever did you come up with that idea?"

"After the native boy stole my idea to use the exotic flower to suck his dick, I noticed a bunch of bees flying around them in the field and that got me thinking..."

Tara nodded, reflecting back on what the old lady had said after Jessop completed his performance.

"The old lady said you've got a good shot at being chosen one of the two winners for the couples' performance later this month," she said.

"That's good, I guess," Jessop chuckled. "But I'll have to come up with something *new* if I am. I don't think the bees or my partner will take very kindly to my sticking my tool covered in insects into her pussy."

"Well, you'd better put your other head to good use in the meantime, because Gisella's planning to work us into the schedule for our own performances soon."

"Yeah," Clover nodded. "And I'm already getting some good ideas about how the two of us can hook up in a way they've never seen before..."

"I can't wait," Jessop grinned. "But right now, I need a little shuteye. After coming harder than I have in a long time, I need some time to rest and recover."

"Me too," Tara said. "I wonder what the next presenter will show us tomorrow? Maybe she'll put a *snake* or something up her pussy. The performances seem to be getting more and more exotic every day."

"I don't know," Clover said. "But I'm getting wet again just thinking about it. Those native girls are crazy-hot."

"Are you sure you don't want to hookup with a *girl* instead of a boy if you're chosen as the second winner?" Tara said. "If you transform into a ladyboy, you can have it either way."

"True," Clover said, sliding her fingers over her dripping pussy and raising them to her mouth to taste her juices. "So many possibilities, so little time..."

The following evening, the trio returned to the theater shortly before dusk, joining Gisella in their customary spot near the front of the stage. While one of the elders lit the candles surrounding the dais, the drummer began his familiar beat, signaling that a new performance was about to begin. When the sun finally set over the mountains, another naked native girl approached the rear of the stage with her hands clasped gently over her muff. Clover peered at the stage, covered only in a collection of soft animal furs, then she glanced back at the pretty girl with empty hands.

"No *props* tonight?" she said to the old lady sitting next to her.

"It doesn't look like it," Gisella nodded.

"After the *rocking horse* and Jessop's *buzz show*, it's hard to imagine anyone bringing something new to the table. There's only so many ways a guy or a girl can bring themselves to climax..."

"Maybe so," Gisella said. "But sometimes less is more. There's nothing quite the same as watching a young person touch their naked bodies for the first time as they learn the pleasures of self-stimulation."

"True," Tara nodded, watching the young girl slowly ascend the stairs and walk out to the middle of the stage. "Especially when they're as beautiful as this one."

"I could get off just watching her *stand* there for the rest of the night," Jessop nodded, stroking his hardening tool while he ran his eyes over the girl's lithe and toned body.

When the drummer pounded the final beat of his drum and the crowd applauded the girl for coming onto the stage, she paused for a moment, then she moved her hands off to the side and lifted her right knee, slowly straightening her leg and angling it upward over her head.

"Wow," Clover gasped. "That's some pretty impressive flexibility."

"No kidding," Tara nodded, watching the girl stretching her legs into a one-hundred-and-eighty-degree perfect upright angle. "And balance."

"And look at her *pussy*," Jessop panted while staring at her glistening vulva, gaping open from the stretched folds. "I've never seen one exposed quite this way before. What I'd do to be standing in front of her right now–"

"You just might have your chance soon enough," Gisella said, glancing down at his upturned erection, bouncing up over his belly.

While the trio stared in admiration at the girl's sexy figure and her athletic ability, she slowly slid her right hand over the front of her abdomen and inserted three fingers into her hole while she angled her little finger toward her pink rosebud and placed her thumb over her hardening nub, circling it slowly as she jilled herself softly.

"Fuck, that's hot," Clover gushed, sliding three fingers into her own dripping cavity to mimic the action of the girl on the stage.

"You weren't *kidding* when you said less is more," Tara panted, strumming her thumb over her throbbing gland while she stretched her other fingers toward her sphincter. "Just when I thought it couldn't possibly get any sexier..."

"There's something about watching a girl touch her body without any extra aids or tools," Jessop shuddered, stroking his erection even harder as pre-cum began to dribble over the sides of his flaring helmet.

"Especially when she's exposing herself in such an open way," Clover nodded.

The girl fingered her entire exposed perineum while she moaned softly, then she slowly began to shift her foot on the stage, gradually rotating the angle of her body that was facing toward the audience. As her pretty ass and upturned leg started to quiver in rising excitement, the crowd nodded appreciatively while they stroked their own naked figures in matching excitement.

"Holy shit," Tara shuddered as she slid her fingers over her slippery slit. "She looks even *more* gorgeous from the other side."

"That ass is to die for," Jessop nodded, humping his hips harder in the air while he imagined fucking her from behind.

"I call first dibs," Clover grunted, thrusting her fingers deep into her tunnel, up to her knuckles. "Especially if I get called up as the winner on the *boys'* side."

"No fair," Jessop said, turning to glare at his friend with tilted eyebrows. "You get to show *both sides* of your gender when you transform into a ladyboy!"

"You could have had a chance, too," Clover smiled. "Who's to say that the magic crystals only work on a *girl*?"

"Can you two shut up for a moment while I concentrate on this girl's performance?" Tara moaned, watching the girl on the stage begin to bend over at the waist and lower her chest onto her lower leg while tilting her other leg straight up in the opposite direction.

"What the fuck?" Clover gasped, staring at the girl's

perfect upside-down split as the toes of her left leg quivered in the air.

"I think she's getting close to climaxing," Jessop nodded, stroking his dick harder.

"Yes," Tara groaned, sliding her fingers deeper into her hole, along with all the other women watching the performance. "Her face is reddening and her tits are starting to shake—"

"And look at the *stream of juices* pouring out of her slit, all the way down her leg toward her mouth," Jessop said.

"Fuck, I can't hold it any longer," Clover grunted, pushing her hand all the way into her hole and squirting her juices all over Gisella's legs and her friend's shaking bodies.

Suddenly, a thick spray squirted out of the performer's pussy, spraying in every direction around the curved auditorium while she shuddered and struggled to maintain her balance in her upside-down, one-legged stance. The entire auditorium moaned in unison, equally mesmerized by the athletic girl's erotic performance. When she finally stopped shaking and squirting, the girl tilted her torso upward and lowered her raised leg, turning around to face the crowd with her glistening hands once again placed softly overtop of her dripping mound. As the audience rose to give her a standing ovation, Clover, Tara, and Jessop had to be careful not to slip on the puddles of fluid they'd each left on the step between their legs while they clapped along enthusiastically.

"Wow," Clover said, nodding her head excitedly. "That's one I've never seen before."

"Yeah," Tara panted. "I can't wait to plant my face between your legs in that position."

"Not if *I* get there first," Jessop said, his dick still bobbing and leaking over his glistening belly.

"Well, while you guys *wrestle* it out," Gisella chuckled. "I've got to finish the schedule for the rest of the month. With only a handful of performers left to present before the next full moon, it's going to be a tight competition to see who comes out on top."

"Not to mention who comes out on top later *tonight*," Jessop chuckled, winking at his friends.

3

____

When the three friends returned to their cabin after the show, they were so excited, they jumped into bed immediately, rubbing their bodies together. It didn't take long for Clover and Tara to become tangled up scissoring their hips, and while Clover lay on her back, lifting one knee over her shoulder, Tara angled her body overtop of her, splaying her legs like the girl on the stage had done, grinding their slippery vulvas together.

"As much as I love watching the two of you rubbing your cunnies together," Jessop grunted, growing increasingly aroused watching them rocking their bodies in tandem. "I'm feeling a little left out of the action."

"It might not be as easy for you to slide your dick between our pussies in this position," Clover said, peering up at him with a flushed face. "But if you sit on my chest facing toward Tara, you can slide your hard-on between my breasts while you lick Tara's tits at the same time."

"That might work," Jessop smiled, kneeling over Clover's shoulders and tilting his ass upward toward her face as he positioned his erection between her shaking breasts and mashed them together while he slathered Tara's tits with his tongue.

"Mmm," Tara moaned, angling her body in his direction while she pressed her pussy down harder over Clover's dripping slit. "I guess you got your wish to rub your dick against a pretty girl's body tonight after all."

"It wasn't exactly what I had in mind," Jessop chuckled, sliding his hands over Clover's slippery belly and massaging her leaking juices over her compressed breasts and his sliding tool. "But two girls is always better than one."

Clover tilted her head upward for a moment, watching Jessop's ass rocking between her slippery tits.

"This is pretty hot watching you from this angle," she grunted. "I can see your balls tightening and your anus puckering with every thrust."

"Feel free to *lick* it if you're in the mood," Jessop panted. "I washed myself thoroughly before the show, so it should be squeaky clean."

"I don't mind if I *do*," Clover smiled, raising her head a few inches higher and extending her tongue to tease the rim of Jessop's flexing sphincter while he rocked his hips harder and buried his face in Tara's shaking breasts.

"Fuckkkk," Jessop groaned when he felt Clover's warm tongue bathing his butthole.

"You like that?" Clover huffed, feeling the pressure in her hips rapidly escalating while Tara cunt-fucked her in the open-scissor position.

"God, yes," Jessop rasped, biting Tara's swelling nipples as he felt the familiar sensation of his tingling balls. "I can't hold it any longer–*unghhh!*"

When Clover felt Jessop shooting over her belly and saw his pucker spasming in simultaneous contractions, she lost all control over her rising pleasure, squirting her juices out every side of her mashed pussy. Meanwhile, Tara, who had been enjoying Jessop's stimulation of her nipples, wrapped her arms tightly around his head and squeezed him in a bear hug while she gushed her own juices in a torrent toward his spurting tool. While the trio held onto each other in a tight mutual embrace, they moaned loudly together, jerking their bodies in unison until each of them finished squirting, falling down next to each other in a trembling jumble.

"You have to admit," Clover panted from the bottom of the pile. "These erotic shows are certainly giving us lots of new ways to broaden our sex life."

"Not to mention putting us in the mood for these nightly liaisons," Tara chuckled. "I haven't come this often and this hard since we left the erotic temple of Sannyans..."

"Somehow, this is even sexier than getting it on with those erotic sculptures," Jessop nodded. "There's something about watching these young people pleasure themselves for the first time–"

"I'm pretty sure that isn't the *first* time they've explored their sexuality," Clover smiled. "Waiting until you're eighteen to touch yourself is a pretty difficult task. Judging by the creativity and skill they bring to some of their routines, I suspect they've had plenty of practice beforehand."

"Maybe so," Jessop said. "But doing it in front of the whole crowd adds a whole new layer of excitement to the experience."

"I wonder if the rest of the tribe is going back to their cabins and trying out some of these techniques like we are," Tara said. "They certainly seem to be getting just as turned on watching the performers..."

"Maybe it's their way of bottling up the youngsters'

hormones for their own pleasure. They must get plenty turned on running around naked all day long staring at everyone else's bodies."

"Possibly," Tara said. "Either way, they're come up with a genius idea for stretching the boundaries and encouraging further sexual exploration. I never knew there could be so many ways to get off by stimulating yourself."

"I wonder what the next performer will do to raise the bar higher?" Jessop said, stroking his dripping tool absent-mindedly.

Clover grinned, watching his dick twitching against his thigh.

"Are you getting more aroused watching the *guys* or the *girls*?" she said.

"I don't know if I'm getting quite as turned on by the men's performances," Jessop smiled. "But I'm certainly getting a lot of new ideas for how I can pleasure myself when you guys aren't available."

The following night, the three friends joined Gisella in the amphitheater before the drummer finished his introductory crescendo, signaling the start of a new erotic performance. This time though, they noticed a thin, translucent screen made of loosely woven cloth covering the front of the stage, and they peered at the old lady with a quizzical expression.

"Aren't we going to see the performer *naked* tonight?" Clover said, pinching her eyebrows in disappointment.

"I suspect he'll be nude alright," Gisella nodded, watching the outline of a tall native youth strolling toward the back of the stage against the backlight of the flickering candles. "Maybe he's just going to tease us for a little bit while we wait for the big finale."

"That's okay," Tara grunted when she saw the youth rise up from the top of the stairs, revealing his muscular torso and rounded hips in the silhouette of the surrounding candles.

"Jesus," Jessop gasped, staring at the large swinging pendulum between his legs. "Is that actually his *dick* hanging between his legs?"

"That's where it usually is," Tara chuckled, flaring her eyes as she stared at the python snaking down the side of one thigh.

"If that's what it looks like in a *semi-flaccid* state," Clover shuddered. "I can't wait to see what it looks like angry."

The youth stepped forward a few inches and swiped his swelling phallus from side to side against the soft fabric of the curtain, slowly tenting it outward until it appeared that he was levitating an instrument the size of an axe handle between his muscular legs.

"Holy shit," Tara gasped. "That can't be real. I've never seen a dick that big before..."

Suddenly, the youth pulled his body away from the front of the curtain and turned it sideways, showing the full outline of his figure in side profile. His huge erection stood proudly upward in a forty-five degree angle, bobbing gently above his equally enormous balls.

"That's an erect penis alright," Clover panted, slipping her hand between her legs and inserting two fingers into her throbbing cavity. "There's no mistaking that shape and contour."

"I'd love to wrap my *lips* around that contour," Tara grunted, rubbing her slippery slit while she fantasized about fucking the hung tribesman. "Whichever pair could fit him inside me."

"Look at that *ass*," Clover nodded while she thrust her fingers deeper into her dripping hole. "That is one seriously fuckable derriere. Maybe *Jessop* would prefer a turn with this one–"

"I'd rather feel that huge flagpole in my hands," Jessop nodded, stroking his fully erect dick with both hands. "I'd love to watching him shoot off while I squeeze those big balls of his."

"Yes," Tara hissed, watching the youth tilt his torso downward until it was resting atop his thighs, with his foot-long erection pointed downward below his baseball-sized nutsac. "Now *that's* a picture I won't soon forget. I'd milk that cow any day..."

"He can shoot his cream on me anytime," Clover nodded, rocking her hips harder on the cold concrete step of the amphitheater while she fucked her pussy harder.

"But why isn't he *touching* himself?" Jessop said, wrinkling his forehead as he stroked his cock in rising pleasure. "He certainly looks aroused enough."

"Maybe he's just trying to get us in the mood," Gisella smiled, stroking her own slippery slit while she watched the adonis showing off for the audience.

"Well, if that's his intent, it's certainly working," Clover shuddered. "I don't know if I'll be able to hold off long enough to see him coming for himself..."

But just as the three friends began to feel themselves reaching their bursting point, the hung youth lifted his body and turned around, swiping the tip of his erection against the front of the curtain, swiping it from side to side as his enormous phallus stretched the fabric a few inches above the platform.

"Okay," Clover gushed silently. "At this point, I'd be happy to come back simply as that swinging *curtain* in my next life–"

"I think he needs something a little warmer and tighter to finish the job," Tara grunted, jilling herself harder as a steady stream of liquid dripped out of her gaping pussy and down the crack of her ass.

"It's a shame he's keeping that thing hidden behind the curtain," Jessop nodded as his pre-cum coated the entire surface of his throbbing glans, adding an extra layer of lubrication for his fapping tool. "I bet he could make everybody come just by displaying it in its full glory."

As if on cue, the young tribal boy angled his bobbing tool toward the center of the curtain, then he pulled the two sides apart along a small hidden slit, thrusting his enormous erection through the hole, showing it glistening and bobbing atop of the candles flickering at the front of the stage.

"Oh my God," Clover gasped, feeling her pussy lips beginning to spasm against her embedded fingers in a mini-orgasm. "It even bigger than I imagined!"

"Not to mention *prettier*," Tara nodded, jerking her hands furiously inside her leaking cunt. "Just look at the beautiful flared head."

"It's dripping like a faucet," Jessop groaned, feeling his own cock becoming more slippery by the moment from his leaking pre-cum. "Why doesn't he *touch* himself and let the rest of us get off with him?"

"He seems to be enjoying the process of teasing us with his impressive instrument almost as much," Gisella said, slipping her fingers into her slit as her eyes widened, along with the rest of the crowd.

Suddenly, the youth arched his hips upward as he

caressed his tightening balls against the front of the curtain, and his big dick bounced excitedly up and down while he shot one long, thick rope of cum after another over the lip of the stage, splattering over the hard marble floor of the amphitheater. The friends lost count of how many jets he spurted outward, mesmerized by his pulsating organ and throbbing crown as he moaned softly behind the billowing curtain, yawning his mouth open while he gasped in ecstasy.

"Unghh," Clover groaned, shaking her hips violently on the edge of the stair while she squirted all over her trembling hips and hands.

"Hissst..." Tara hissed in turn, coming equally hard sitting next to her.

"Gah!" Jessop grunted, shooting long strings of cum between his quivering legs while he choked his dick like his life depended on it.

"Mmmm," Gisella purred, squeezing her thighs tightly over her shaking hands, embedded between her legs.

"Fuck, that was hot," Clover said when she finally finished coming. "He didn't even *touch* himself the whole time..."

"He didn't have to," Gisella said. "Apparently, caressing his erection against the soft fabric of the curtain and knowing everyone was admiring his organ was enough."

"If he can come that hard just by displaying his erection for the benefit of the crowd," Tara nodded. "Can you imagine what would happen if he had a live *body* next to him?"

"You might get your turn soon enough," the old lady smiled.

"Have you been able to work us into the schedule?" Clover said, twisting her head around to peer at Gisella.

"I could only fit one of you in for this month," she nodded. "There's still six more performers scheduled ahead of you. You'll have your chance on the last night before the full moon."

"I don't know if I'll be able to *last* that long," Clover panted while she watched her juices dribbling out of her throbbing pussy onto the cool marble step.

"I guess we'll just have to practice harder in the meantime," Tara chuckled.

"Well, you won't have to worry about the *hard* part," Jessop grunted, swinging his half-erect cock from side to side as it slapped against the sides of his dripping thighs.

"You three do your thing while the rest of us turn in for the night and prepare for another erotic performance tomorrow night," the old lady nodded. "I have a feeling you're going to find the *next* presentation ups the ante one level higher..."

4

———

"Hot damn," Clover said when the three friends returned to their cabin after the show. "That was crazy hot."

"Yeah," Tara nodded. "Who knew it could be so stimulating watching a guy get off without touching himself?"

"Well, technically," Jessop laughed. "He *was* touching himself, albeit with a piece of fabric..."

"Do you think you could come that easily?" Tara said. "You seem to prefer the more direct approach."

"I dunno," Jessop smiled. "I suppose it would depend on how *aroused* I got beforehand..."

Clover paused for a moment while she peered at Tara with a mischievous grin.

"How would you like *us* to put on a little show of our own?" she said. "Lord knows, I'm certainly still in the mood."

"That's not a bad idea," Jessop grinned. "Why don't you compete to see who can put on the more erotic performance? Gisella said only one of you can be slotted in to present later this month. This seems like as good an idea as any to see who should go first."

"I'm game if you are," Clover said, winking at Tara. "Do you have any ideas how we should do it?"

"I could use a bit more practice getting ready for my *self-licking* routine," Tara said. "I've been getting closer to touching myself with my tongue, but I need a little help getting the rest of the way."

"I might be able to help you with that," Clover said, reaching over to her satchel and pulling out the mage's magic crystals. "If we position ourselves the right way, I think I can give you a little extra incentive to push a bit further."

"What exactly did you have in mind?" Tara said, suddenly feeling her pussy twitching again at the thought of hooking up with Clover in her ladyboy guise.

"Why don't you lie down face up in a crouched position with your legs pulled back over your head? Then I'll position myself facing you, with my cock pointed over your vulva. The closer your mouth gets to licking the tip, the further I'll pull back until you can touch your clit."

"That sounds hot," Tara nodded. "But what if I want your *dick* in the mix, too?"

"We might be able to work something out," Clover grinned.

"What about *me*?" Jessop said, furrowing his brow. "What am I supposed to do while you're having all the fun?"

"You can practice your own masturbation technique," Clover chuckled. "You're going to have to come up with something new if you're chosen as the boys' winner for the couples' presentation. Let your mind wander while you watch the two of us. Maybe you'll come up with something equally original."

While the two girls got into position facing one another and Clover rolled the crystals in her hand, Jessop peered around the cabin, looking for something he could use to stimulate himself while he watched. He noticed a silk hand-kerchief lying in Clover's satchel and he picked it up, caressing it against his hardening tool.

"Mmm," Clover said while she watched his erection lifting the fabric higher. "That's getting me in the mood pretty quick, thinking back on that last performance in the theater."

As her clit began to tingle and swell, she glanced between her legs, watching her ladyboy cock gradually growing and lengthening until it was standing fully erect next to Tara's dripping pussy. Tara angled her legs further behind her head, then she placed her palms under the cheeks of her ass, pulling her head closer toward her crotch.

"Give me more of that," she panted while staring at Clover's throbbing tool. "I want to suck that pretty ladyboy cock of yours."

"All in due time," Clover smiled, raising up onto her knees and thrusting her prick between Tara's slippery folds until the glistening tip slid over Tara's pearl.

"Yes," Tara grunted, flexing her spine a few degrees further while her mouth inched closer toward the end of Clover's flaring dick. "I can almost reach it–"

"Not quite yet," Clover grinned, pulling her erection back a few inches, just out of reach.

"You're such a tease," Tara huffed while she focused on Clover's dripping glans like an eagle spotting a slithering snake on the ground.

"This is all about *you* this time," Clover chuckled as she slowly slid her prick back and forth over Tara's dripping slit. "I thought you wanted a bit of extra incentive to stretch your body into a self-sucking position..."

"Well, yes," Tara grunted, tensing her arms tighter as she

tried pulling her pussy closer toward her flapping tongue. "But *you're* supposed to be practicing too. What are you going to do with that pretty boy-cock when you get your chance to perform on the stage?"

"I've got a few ideas," Clover grinned, angling her hips slightly forward and dipping the tip of her organ into Tara's puffy lips.

"Unghh," Tara groaned, trying to angle her hips further upward to press Clover's appendage further into her hole. "That feels good. Fuck me deeper."

"Not yet," Clover smiled, pulling her hard-on out of Tara's slit and pressing her dripping crown closer toward her face. "You're almost there. You've just got a few more inches to go."

"Ssssst," Tara hissed while she stretched her neck until the tip of her tongue touched Clover's glans. "I can taste your pre-come. Give me more."

"Jesus," Jessop grunted from a few feet away while he swiped the silky hankie over his bobbing cock. "That is seriously hot. I haven't been this turned on since I watched the girl with the rocking horse–"

"I'm glad you're enjoying yourself," Clover chuckled. "Just make sure you don't come in my hankie. I don't fancy smelling your spunk every time I have to wipe my nose."

"I'll try not to," Jessop grunted as his cock bounced ever harder while he swiped the soft cloth over his tingling organ. "But I'm getting pretty close..."

"Me too," Clover said, pulling the tip of her throbbing pole away from Tara's flapping tongue while her dick pulsed on the edge of climax.

"No fair!" Tara said, wrinkling her forehead. "I was almost there. Just when this was starting to work..."

"It's working a little *too* well," Clover shuddered, lifting her bouncing hard-on over Tara's slit to keep herself from coming. "This is supposed to be a *solo* demonstration, remember? You've only got another inch or so to reach the prize."

"Mmm," Tara groaned, staring at her pink bulb with her lips pursed in anticipation. "I can almost taste it now."

"Maybe *this* will help," Clover said, placing her hands over the back of Tara's thighs and pushing her into an even tighter crunch.

"Mmmff!" Tara grunted, when her lips finally encircled her burning gland. She pulled her legs further upward and began to suck her bead harder as her face suddenly turned a deep shade of red.

"You did it, babe!" Clover gushed, mesmerized by her friend's self-cunnilingus technique. "How does it feel to be able to such your own clit?"

"Mmmm," Tara nodded excitedly, not wanting to take her lips off her tingling gland for even a moment.

"Fuck, that's insane," Jessop grunted next to them, watching the soft handkerchief flapping over his erection while it bounced up and down like a flagpole in a heavy breeze. "You're right, I didn't even need to touch myself directly to come this time. I can feel my orgasm welling up in my balls–"

"Wait for me," Clover nodded, noticing a flush spreading rapidly over Tara's shaking tits, signaling the imminent pinnacle of her pleasure.

Without waiting a moment longer, she angled her body forward and plunged her prick deep into Tara's quivering pussy, emptying her seed inside her hole while both women gushed their juices over one another's pulsating perineums. When Tara felt Clover gushing inside her, she sucked her gland even harder into her mouth, shaking violently while she groaned in delirious pleasure. Seconds later, Jessop's dick began bobbing wildly as he shot one hard stream of cum after another into the waving handkerchief, arching his head upwards in simultaneous ecstasy.

When the three friends finally stopped shaking and panting, they peered at one another with flushed faces.

"Sorry about that," Jessop said with a sheepish grin. "I couldn't help it. When I saw you dip your dick into Tara's pussy with her face planted over her clit, I couldn't hold it any longer."

"It's alright," Clover panted, pulling her dripping erection out of Tara's hole and peering at her friend while she rested her chin over her glistening mound. "I'm just glad the three of us were able to achieve our mutual goals. I think you should be the next one to perform on the stage this month. That was crazy-hot watching you suck your own pussy."

"It *felt* crazy-hot," Tara nodded. "Even *better* when you came inside me at the same time."

"Who's to say we won't have another chance to try this a different way the next time?" Clover smiled. "When I get a chance to show my stuff on the stage, I could just as easily be chosen the *male* winner. If we play our cards right, I might be the boy and you can be the girl. Then we can show these tribespeople something that will *really* open their eyes."

5

————

The next day, as dusk approached once again, the three friends made their way back to the village amphitheater, where they noticed a strange apparatus set up on the stage. There was a small wooden platform with a series of hollowed-out bamboo poles leading into the top and out the bottom of the tub-shaped object. On the far side of the stage, the bamboo stems were elevated above the platform, and on the near side facing the audience, the tubes were directed off to the side of the dais. Clover peered at the old lady who was waiting for them in their usual spot and squinted her eyes.

"That's an unusual contraption," she said. "How is our next performer planning to use this?"

"You'll just have to wait and see," Gisella smiled. "Half of the fun of these demonstrations is seeing all the different ways our young people have learned to stimulate themselves."

"They've certainly been pretty creative so far," Tara nodded.

"As have you," Gisella said. "I'm looking forward to see

what you girls have got planned for your performances later this month. Have you generated any new ideas?"

"A few," Clover grinned while she winked at Tara. "But we'd rather keep it a surprise until everybody can see it together. I'm pretty sure they won't be disappointed."

"I can't wait," the old lady said, glancing at Jessop. "And how about you, young man? Have you been practicing some of the new techniques you've seen demonstrated on our stage?"

"I have indeed," Jessop nodded.

"And have you thought about some new strategies you might use if you're chosen to perform as part of the couples' demonstration during the full moon?"

"I've come up with a few ideas," he grinned as he peered at Clover and Tara. "With a little help from my roommates."

"Good," Gisella nodded. "Because the competition is growing more fierce every day."

When the sunlight began to fade behind the mountains in the distance, the drummer started his familiar rhythm, slowly pounding the drum harder and faster while another performer approached the rear of the podium. When she stepped onto the flickering platform, the three friends gasped, staring at her sylphlike figure. She was more petite that the other female performers, but that only accentuated her pretty hourglass figure. Her caramel-colored skin radiated in the moonlight, and her blue eyes glimmered in the flickering light of the surrounding candles like a Lorelei luring passing sailors into her trance.

But the part of her appearance that the trio found most alluring was the absence of any body hair. Unlike the other performers, she had shaved her entire body to highlight her perfect figure. As she stepped into the small tub-shaped basin placed in the center of the stage, she waved her body from side to side, slowly turning around while the audience applauded in silent appreciation. The friends could see the light of the candles flickering in the small diamond-shaped space between the top of her thighs, and her pretty nub hanging below her glistening folds like a cherry just waiting to be plucked.

"She's absolutely *gorgeous*," Clover gushed, feeling her own hardening gland pressing out of her tingling folds. "But what is she planning to do with that elaborate apparatus?"

"Something tells me we're about to find out," Gisella nodded, noticing the girl signal toward an aide standing at the side of the stage.

Suddenly, they heard a soft rumbling sound, and the bamboo shafts over the top of the stage began to shake, then a torrent of water began gushing out of the open end positioned over the tub, cascading down over the girl's naked body.

"Oh!" Clover gasped, watching the water splashing over the girl's head and shoulders and streaming down the front of her undulating body as she danced in the waterfall. "That's a little different..."

"It's sexy as *fuck*," Jessop nodded as his tool began to instantly harden. "The water is highlighting every sexy curve and crevasse of her body."

"There's only one crevasse I'm looking at right now," Tara grunted while she played with her clit as she watched the girl turn around and bend over at the waist while the stream of water bounced over her backside and down the crack of her ass, over her gleaming bare pussy.

While the small tub slowly began to fill with water, the overflow spilled out the side into the bamboo pipes directed toward a nearby ditch. With the river of gurgling fluid drizzling off to the side, the girl turned back around to face the audience, then she sat down on a small bench, tilting her head upwards as the falling water splashed off her face and streamed down between her upturned breasts and her separated legs.

"*Damn*," Clover panted, rubbing her clit while she imagined sitting next to the pretty girl under the improvised waterfall. "That's the sexiest shower I've seen in a long time."

"It was very thoughtful of her to set one up for all of us to witness," Tara grinned.

"It looks very stimulating," Jessop nodded, watching the girl spread her legs further apart while the torrent of water streamed over her tilted hips. "But will she be able to come just from the flow of water running between her legs?"

"She seems to be getting pretty *close*," Tara nodded, watching the girl's body starting to quiver as she positioned the cascade over her glistening bulb and her separating folds.

When she began rubbing her pussy with one hand and squeezing one of her breasts with the other, it became increasingly obvious that she was building toward an imminent climax. As the water splashed over her tilted head and shaking tits, she gaped her lips open, allowing the cascade to fill her mouth and spill down the front of her bosom, creating an even stronger stream sliding down the valley of her parted thighs.

"Fuck me," Clover grunted as she felt her own juices gushing down the middle of her slit and over the crack of her ass. "What I'd do to be rubbing my pussy against hers right now in that sexy waterfall."

"Screw using my *pussy*," Tara groaned. "I'd be happy to plant my *face* between her legs while I she gave my own special facial–"

"Something tells me she could use a *cock* right about

now," Jessop said as the girl slipped two fingers inside her hole and squirted the spraying water over the insides of her thighs.

"That's fucking hot," Clover moaned, feeling the pressure between her thighs building toward the bursting point. "I think she's going to come soon..."

While the girl on the stage jilled her pussy harder with her hand between her legs, she squeezed her breast tighter and spread her mouth open wider while she stared at the crowd with blinking eyelashes. When she suddenly began jerking her body in violent spasms and loud moans, the rest of the group groaned in unison as they touched themselves and climaxed in a synchronized hum surrounding the large amphitheater. While the three friends flapped their legs in and out in cresting pleasure, the old lady sat perfectly still as she quivered her body sitting next to them with her hands embedded between her clasping thighs.

When the girl on the stage finally stopped groaning and shaking under the improvised waterfall, she tilted her body backwards a few degrees further, relishing the sensation of the warm fluid sliding over her body. Clover peered over at the old lady, noticing her flushed face and her hands positioned tightly between her legs.

"You seem to be enjoying this almost as much as the rest of us," she smiled. "Did you have your own turn on the stage when you were our age?"

"We *all* did," Gisella nodded. "It's one of the ways we've been able to keep our sex lives fresh and exciting all these years. The young people are always coming up with adventurous new ways to stimulate themselves, which have been adopted by the rest of the tribe."

"What did you do when you were on the stage, if you

don't mind my asking?" Tara said, squinting at the old lady curiously.

"I don't want to ruin the secret," she grinned. "Maybe I'll tell you after you girls finish your presentation later this month. I wouldn't want to influence what you've already got planned."

"That seems to be constantly evolving," Clover laughed. "Every time we see another performer demonstrating a new technique, we keep revising our technique."

"Glad to hear that you're broadening your horizons," Gisella said. "I'm getting almost as excited anticipating what you're going to bring to the table as I am about our next group of young performers."

"We hope we don't disappoint you," Tara nodded, smiling at the old lady. "If we can retain even *half* of your energy and sexual curiosity when we reach your age, this whole experience will have paid for itself many times over."

6

————

After the erotic performance of the girl in the homemade waterfall, Clover, Tara, and Jessop returned to their cabin, exhausted but still sticky from their self-stimulation while watching the show. At first light, they ventured into the forest and found a nearby waterfall, frolicking under the warm spray while rubbing their bodies together to enjoy a series of powerful climaxes. Then they went for a swim in the lagoon at the base of the cataract, lying in the soft grass at the edge of the embankment for a long, relaxing nap. On their way back to the village, they found some strange trees with a diagonal slice on the side of their bark, with large pails positioned under the bottom of the slice to collect its white sap.

Tara walked up to one of the trees and peered inside the bucket, dipping her finger into the creamy liquid and raising it to her mouth.

"Ugh," she said, spitting the resin onto the ground with a twisted face. "That stuff's definitely not *edible*. At least in this raw condition."

Clover strolled up next to her and lowered her face toward the edge of the bucket, inhaling its pungent odor.

"That smell is familiar," she nodded. "Like something we used to have in the land where I came from."

"Whatever could you use this disgusting *goo* for?" Tara said, wrinkling her forehead.

Clover placed her fingers into the bucket and raised a cupful in her cupped hands. She pulled the tacky substance between her fingers, noticing it stretching and thinning before it fell back into the pail.

"It appears to be a kind of *rubber*," she said. "We used to make various useful objects from this substance once its properly cured. Automobile tires, elastic bands, even men's condoms–"

"I have no idea what any of these things are," Tara said, shaking her head.

Jessop joined the two girls and dipped his hand into the bucket next to Clover's, pinching his eyebrows together in curiosity.

"It's slippery and feels kind of *doughy*," he nodded. "What happens to it when it dries and cures?"

"It becomes firmer and stretchier," Clover said. "It can be quite a useful substance in the right circumstances."

"So I'm beginning to see," Jessop smiled as he rolled his fingers softly together. "Something tells me these tribespeople have developed their own special uses for it..."

When the trio returned to the village, they helped out in the fields for a little while, then they joined the rest of the villagers in the central square for the evening feast. After filling their stomachs with venison stew and home-brewed ale, they joined Gisella and the rest of the tribe in the big amphitheater as dusk settled over the courtyard. When they took their spot near the front of the stage, they noticed a large hump on the platform, covered by one of the soft animal skins.

"Another prop for tonight's performance?" Clover smiled at the old lady.

"So it would seem," Gisella nodded.

As the drummer began picking up the pace of his drumbeat, the group noticed another figure approaching the rear of the stage.

"I'm looking forward to this one," Tara grinned, feeling her heartbeat pounding in tandem with the rhythm of the drum. "It's time for the boys to do their thing again. I can't wait to see what he's cooked up this time."

"Judging by the size of the object on the stage," Gisella smiled. "It appears that he's been pretty busy concocting his own kind of aphrodisiac..."

The youth walked up the steps at the rear of the dais, then he paused in front of the covered object, resting his hands by his side while the crowd admired his buff and lean figure. He was more slender than the other young tribesmen, bending one knee in a tilted posture, appearing slightly effeminate. Then he leaned over and gently lifted the cloak of the concealed object, eliciting a gasp from the audience. The object was shaped in the form of a person's ass, complete with a puckering sphincter in the center of the crack separating the perfectly round cheeks.

"That's quite an impressive sculpture," Clover nodded, squinting closer at the surface of the pink-colored bust. "It looks very soft."

"It is," the old lady nodded as she watched the youngster run the fingers of his hand down the middle of the crack, pausing for a moment while he played with the realistic-looking anus.

"Is that made out of the same stuff we saw being harvested from the trees in the forest?"

"So it would seem," Gisella nodded.

"How did he shape it into that spongy texture and make it *flesh-colored*?"

"With the right mix of plant dyes and curing in the sun, the firmness and color of the substance can be easily adjusted."

"That's *ingenious*," Jessop said, feeling his own dick hardening while he imagined using it for his own private pleasure. "But I'm looking forward to seeing what the *other* side looks like."

As if on cue, the young tribesman squatted down on his knees and slowly turned the basket-sized mold around, revealing a surprise twist in the design. Instead of having the smooth surface of a woman's mound and a narrow slit running between the top of her carved thighs, a large, fleshy phallus in the shape of an erect cock pointed upwards from the front of the bust. While it was only a partial representation of a man's midsection, cut off from roughly the top of his belly button to a few inches below his joined thighs, it otherwise appeared to be an anatomically perfect replica of a man's lower body, albeit with a full inflamed erection.

"That's incredible," Clover gushed, feeling her pussy twitching while she dreamed about using the improved sex doll for her own amusement. "How did he create such a natural shape out of that soft liquid?"

"It appears that he had plenty of time to carve a reverse

mold in the shape of a man's midsection," Gisella said. "Once the sap is poured into a carved wooden bowl, it takes on the shape of its exterior, slowly hardening to the desired firmness."

"Well, that upturned dick on the *front* of it seems to be quite a bit firmer than the rest of it," Tara chuckled as she watched the youth swatting the upturned phallus playfully from side to side.

"I have a feeling he use some *other* kind of other thickening agent to supplement that part of the anatomy," the old lady smiled.

Suddenly, the young man placed both of his hands around the shaft of the pole, then he pumped his hands slowly up and down while the rubbery coating slipped over the tip of the phallus, revealing a shiny, glistening tip in the shape of a man's helmet-shaped glans.

"Holy fuck!" Tara gasped. "It even moves like a man's hard-on, *foreskin* and all."

"That's one impressive hard-on," Clover nodded. "I'd fuck that dildo any day of the week."

"Something tells me he's got his *own* plans for it," Jessop chuckled, watching the youngster lower his face closer to the top of the swinging instrument, then wrapping his lips around its tip and bobbing his head softly down over its shaft.

Tara shifted her body excitedly on the edge of the step, feeling the cold marble surface suddenly becoming slippery.

"This is the first time we've seen a *homo-erotic* type of self-stimulation," she panted. "Does your tribe encourage and allow same-sex coupling between the tribal members?"

"Yes," Gisella said. "We encourage any kind of sexual

exploration, as long as it is fully consensual and no one is harmed in the process."

"Well," I don't think anyone's going to be harmed by *this* demonstration," Clover chuckled. "Although I suspect that inanimate object is about to be subject to its *own* form of abuse soon enough."

After the youth had coated the faux hard-on with his saliva, he lifted his mouth off the gleaming pole, then he raised his body up and slowly squatted down over the tip of the swinging phallus. An audible groan could be heard coming from the four corners of the amphitheater as the young man sank the artificial pole deep into his ass while the like-minded members of the community jerked their own hardening erections and fingered their tingling anuses in turn.

"Fuck, that's hot," Tara groaned, flicking her own flaring clit while she watched the young man bob his body up and down over the hard rubber bust as his cheeks started to redden.

"He's certainly not *shy*, I'll give you that," Clover grunted, sliding her clit between her fingers while she squeezed one of her tits tightly with her other hand.

"I find it strangely erotic," Jessop nodded, stroking his bobbing tool as he stared at the youth's bouncing erection while he fucked the homemade sex doll shamelessly.

"Yes," Clover shuddered, poking two fingers into her dripping slit while she rocked her hips on the smooth marble step of the stadium. "It's always fun to watch two guys going at it, especially when one of them is swinging his dick in the air for the rest of us to see."

"It looks like he's not going to *finish* that way though," Tara said, pausing her jilling action as the young tribesman stopped rocking atop the truncated statue and suddenly stood up over the swinging phallus. Then he peered up at the audience with a mischievous grin and squatted back down next to the figure, this time with his cock pressed up against the back of its perfectly carved ass. He placed his hands around the sides of the molded bust and raised it upward a few inches above his bobbing erection, then he positioned his glistening glans next to the puckering entrance of the effigy's anus. Much to the surprise and delight of the moaning audience, as he lowered the bust back down over his hips, his tool slipped into the crease of the backside, slowly disappearing into the carved cheeks of the mold.

"Oh my God!" Tara panted. "He's carved a hole in the bust's ass!"

"Yes," Clover groaned, jerking her fingers harder into her hole while she stared, mesmerized, at the sexy youth fucking his perfect partner. "And it appears to be well *lubricated...*"

"The wonders of aloe vera," Gisella nodded as she circled her fingers softly over her own hardening clit.

"I could use some of that for *myself* right now," Jessop grunted, sitting next to the old lady while he stroked his upturned erection with two hands. "I've got to get me one of those pretty sex dolls for my own amusement some time. Do you think that boy might show me how to make own of my own sometime?"

"He even might let you use his personal body, if you ask him politely," the old lady smiled. "Or use his *own* hole for your amusement, if you prefer."

"I normally prefer a *woman's* pussy for that sort of thing," Jessop nodded as he stared down at his rapidly chafing organ while he rubbed it harder. "I find it considerably warmer and wetter for my tastes–"

"Do you need a little *natural* lubrication to assist with that?" Gisella said, swiping her fingers over her moistening slit and rubbing them softly over Jessop's flaring crown.

"Yes, thank you," Jessop groaned as his hands began to slide more effortlessly over his throbbing tool.

"*Look,* Jess," Clover chuckled as she watched her friend becoming more and more aroused watching the erotic performance of the youth on the stage. "He's stroking the doll's dick just like you are now. Maybe when you ask him to hook up, he'll service you from *both* sides at the same time."

"Very funny," Jessop grunted, squeezing his dick even harder, until his crown started to turn a deep shade of purple. "But I prefer to be the *bottom*, thank you very much."

"So does *he*, it would seem," Tara said, noticing the young tribesman picking up the pace of his rocking of the doll over his hips while he stroked and squeezed its upturned erection equally enthusiastically.

"It looks like he's getting close to the tipping point," Clover panted, watching the youth arch his spine backwards and tilt his head upwards as his mouth began to gape open in rising pleasure. "It's too bad we won't be able to see him shooting off when he comes–"

Suddenly, the youth grunted loudly, and his body began to shake in rhythmic convulsions as the artificial cock he was stroking from the back side of the doll began squirting large pulses of cream out the tip of its indented glans in long streams of arcing rope.

"Holy *fuck*," Tara gasped, gushing her own juices out of her contracting hole as her eyes flared open watching the spectacle on the stage. "He seems to have rigged the doll so the hole in its ass is connected to the slit in its phallus. That is the craziest and sexiest thing I've ever seen!"

"No kidding," Clover shuddered, shaking alongside her

while her own juices jetted out of her hole and over the sides of her shaking thighs. "Can you imagine all the things we could do with that sex doll if we had one of our own?"

"Don't worry," Jessop groaned as he squirted one long rope of cum over his and Gisella's quivering thighs while they stared at the sexy youth on the stage having the most intense climax of his life. "I'm already all over it."

7

"That was pretty hot," Clover said when the three friends returned to their room.

"Yeah," Tara nodded, wiping the juices streaming down the insides of her inner thighs. "These young native people have got quite a fertile imagination. What are they going to dream up next?"

"I dunno," Clover smiled. "But now that I know how they make sex toys out of the rubber they grow from their native trees, my mind is already dreaming up some new possibilities."

"It's definitely interesting," Jessop said, staring at the girls' glistening pussies. "But I still prefer the real thing over a fake pussy."

"Or fake *anus*, as the case may be," Tara chuckled.

"It's still kind of weird, watching a guy fucking a man's ass," Jessop said, twisting his face into a queazy frown.

"I bet you wouldn't know the difference if you were *blindfolded*," Clover said. "With the right amount of lube and a tight enough pocket, your cock probably would be equally happy either way."

"Oh, I'm pretty sure I could tell the difference," Jessop laughed.

"Really?" Clover said, raising one eyebrow. "Why don't we *test* it and see for ourselves?"

Jessop paused for a moment while he peered at his two friends suspiciously.

"I'm game if you are," he grinned. "What did you have in mind, exactly?"

"How about if Tara and I bend over side-by-side and present our asses for you?" Clover said. "Each of us will slather our backsides with plenty of aloe vera cream, so you can't tell the difference in the holes based on how wet they are. We'll direct you into one orifice while blindfolded, then another, and you can tell us which you prefer."

"That sounds weird, but strangely hot," Jessop said, his twitching cock betrayed his rising level of excitement. "Bring it on."

"But where are you going to find all this aloe vera cream?" Tara said, squinting at Clover.

"I noticed some plants growing in the woods not too far from our cabin," Clover nodded. "I've been wanting to try this so-called miracle lube that Gisella's been talking about for some time now. Come on, let's go gather some up."

The two girls scampered outside the cabin, then they found for a small green plant with long, spiny leaves, cutting four spongy fronds off with Tara's hunting knife. When they returned to the cabin, Jessop was already standing with his cock at half-mast and his eyes covered with a makeshift bandana.

"Will *this* suit your purposes?" he said when he heard his friends returning.

"I think so," Clover said, sneaking up next to him and testing the tightness of the bandana over his eyes to make sure there were no gaps for him to peek out of. Then she slapped his waving woodie and chuckled. "But I think you're going to need to be a bit *harder* if we're going to test this properly."

Tara sliced the tip off one of the aloe vera shoots, then she squeezed the leaf, watching a white, gelatinous cream oozing out the top.

"Do you want to get the process started?" Clover grinned at her friend.

Tara nodded with a mischievous look on her face, then she applied two generous dollops of the cream in each hand, walking in front of Jessop's bobbing instrument and gripping it tightly with both hands.

"How does that feel, Jessop?" she smiled at Jessop. "Is it as warm and slippery as a woman's pussy?"

Jessop pumped his hips back and forth a few times, then he groaned loudly.

"I can't tell the difference," he grunted. "Does that stuff really come from a *plant*?"

"It does indeed," Clover smiled. "It looks like your little sucking plant isn't the only vegetation you can use for your own amusement."

"Mmm," Jessop nodded as he swung his hips more rapidly. "I could get used to this stuff pretty quickly."

"Well, don't get too excited," Tara chuckled, removing her hands from Jessop's erect boner slapping against his stomach. "We wouldn't want you popping off before you've had a chance to feel a couple of *other* warm places to plant your package."

"Yes, please," Jessop panted, thrusting his hips forward as he eagerly anticipated fucking each of the girls. "Who wants to go first?"

"I'll try it," Clover said, nodding toward Tara. "While I

bend over, you direct his tool toward whichever hole you prefer. Then we'll reverse positions, and I'll direct him toward your other hole. But no touching with your hands. We don't want you cheating to figure out which side of our ass you're fucking."

"No worries," Jessop laughed. "I'm pretty sure my cock will be happy either way. Just let me know if I'm hurting you."

"Okay," Clover said, bending over at the waist and grabbing her ankles while she peered upward between her parted legs. "Let's do this."

Tara glanced at her parted cheeks, then she slathered thick layers of aloe cream all the way up her crack from the base of her mound to the top of her stretching pucker.

"That should do the trick," she grinned, glancing upward at her other friend. "Are you ready, Jessop?"

"My *dick* sure as hell is," he smiled, bouncing his hard-on up and down excitedly.

"Alright," Tara said as she grabbed hold of his tip and pointed it slowly toward Clover's glistening ass. "Let's see where we want to start..."

She pulled Jessop's organ closer to Clover's upturned backside, flapping it up and down a few times to disorient him, then she placed the tip of his organ into Clover's slit, being careful to make sure Jessop kept his hands behind his back.

"Unghh," Jessop groaned as he sank his hard-on deeper into her folds. "That's a familiar sensation. If slightly wetter and creamier than usual..."

"Do you like it better with the extra lubrication?" Clover grunted, squeezing her pussy tighter.

"Maybe," he grinned. "It certainly *sounds* sexier than usual."

"That's from you slapping your balls against my ass," Clover nodded. "Do you like that feeling?"

"Fuck yes," Jessop hissed, driving his pole deeper into Clover's tunnel. "What about you? Am I hurting you?"

"Not yet," Clover panted. "Just try not to thrust too hard. You're pretty well hung, and there's no saying what kind of damage you might do if you ram me all the way to the end..."

"I can feel my balls starting to tingle," Jessop grunted. "I'm going to come pretty soon if we keep this up–"

"We better stop this part of the test then," Tara said, grabbing hold of Jessop's hips with both hands and tensing her muscles to stop his thrusting. "Why don't you pull out while you're still fully hard so you can try it in the next cavity?"

"Okay," Jessop smiled. "But I'm pretty sure what that one was, even if it was a little bit tighter than usual."

"We'll have to see after you have your turn with *my* hole," Tara grinned as Clover stood back up and winked at her.

This time, it was Tara's turn to position herself in front of Jessop's flapping tool, as she leaned over at the waist, clasping her ankles tightly.

"Are you ready for another swing at the plate?" Clover said, grabbing hold of Jessop's swelling glans and squeezing it firmly.

"Definitely," Jessop groaned as a drop of pre-cum spilled out of the tip of his crown. "I'm dying to empty my load into whatever orifice you prefer."

"Alright," Clover nodded, swinging his dick up and down a few inches away from Tara's crack while she slathered another load of aloe vera cream all over her dripping perineum. "Let's see which of these you prefer..."

She pulled Jessop's prick closer toward's Tara's upturned ass, then Tara tilted her hips upwards a few inches to make it seem that Jessop was pointing toward the usual hole.

When his glans pressed against her pucker, she relaxed her sphincter to enable easier access, then Jessop pressed his tool inside her cavity, groaning deeply.

"You like?" Tara grunted as she felt Jessop's thick instrument stretching her apart.

"Damn right," Jessop hissed, shaking his hands behind his back as he sank his dick deeper into Tara's butthole.

"Can you tell the difference yet?" Clover said, standing next to her two friends while she watched Jessop fucking Tara's backside.

"Not really," he said. "They're both equally tight and wet. What about you, Tara?"

"I'm enjoying it as much as always," Tara moaned, surprised at how good it felt to be fucked up the ass by Jessop's big prick.

"Good," Jessop huffed, because it won't take long for me to come at this rate. "I don't know if it's the slipperiness of this new lube, or the tightness of your tunnels that's doing the trick, but I'm going to blast my load any second now."

"Let it go, babe," Tara nodded, slipping one hand over her mound and jilling her clit hard while Jessop pounded her ass. "Let's see if we can come together."

As Jessop's face tightened the closer he inched toward climax, suddenly he rammed his hips forward while he planted his pulsing hard-on all the way inside her hole. As his legs began to buckle and his buttocks quivered in bursting pleasure, he tilted his head all the way back, savoring the pulsating sensation of Tara's contracting anus over the base of his cock while she gushed her juices all over his tight balls. When they both finished shaking and squirting, Jessop pulled his dripping dick out of Tara's ass and turned his face toward Clover, who had come equally hard watching his friends fucking each other like there was no tomorrow.

"Can I take the bandana off now?" he said to Clover.

"Sure," she said, untying the knot at the back of his head and lifting the screen over his eyes.

Jessop peered down at Tara's upturned ass which was still slathered in cream, noticing the streams of clearer liquid streaming down the insides of her thighs.

"So?" Clover grinned, peering down at Tara's sexy ass, while watching Jessop's eyes flaring in surprise. "Could you tell the difference which of our holes you were fucking each time?"

"I honestly can't be sure," Jessop nodded, staring at Tara's glistening slit, still dribbling juices out of its opening. "But judging by how much Tara was gushing over my balls when she came, that had to have been a *pussy* orgasm she was experiencing..."

"Wrong again, bucko," Tara smiled as she peered upward at Jessop between her parted legs. "That was definitely my ass you were fucking this time."

"But how did you–" Jessop said, shaking his head.

"It turns out that your asshole is filled with almost as many nerve endings as the rest of our private parts," Tara grinned, standing up and wiping off the juices that had sprayed over her face when she climaxed in her bent-over position. "You should try it sometime. Clover and I will be happy to return the favor with a homemade dildo made out of hardened rubber. With a bit of extra lube, you might enjoy it just as much as the other boys seem to–"

"Or the *girls*," Clover laughed. "Maybe our next performer will show us a *new* way to play with a dildo."

8

As dusk approached the following day, the three friends returned to the village square and joined Gisella on the front steps of the amphitheater. This time, there was another new apparatus arranged on the stage, looking like a piece of equipment in a children's playground. It consisted of a thick round log, supported by two buttressed columns on each end, raised about chest height over the base of the dais. But affixed to the middle of the log, rested a slightly curved wooded dowel, about six inches long and pointing downward.

"That's a strange-looking *monkey bar*," Clover said, squinting at the mysterious contraption.

"A *what*?" Gisella said, wrinkling her forehead at Clover.

"It's a piece of equipment children used to play with where I come from," Clover nodded.

"Well, I assure you," the old lady chuckled. "This is definitely designed for *adult* use only. Albeit young adults, mostly."

"Any hints as to how our new performer is planning to

use it?" Tara said, wrinkling her brow in curiosity. "If that thing in the middle of the beam is meant to act as a dildo, isn't it pointing in the wrong direction?"

"Your guess is as good as mine," Gisella said. "Our young people are always dreaming up new ideas for stimulating themselves in different ways."

After the candles were illuminated on the stage and the drummer started his familiar drumbeat, the shadow of a naked tribesgirl moved toward the back of the stage. When she climbed up onto the platform, she walked toward the long parallel beam, stopping a few inches away from the hanging phallus pointed between her plump, upturned breasts. Her tits were bigger than most of the other tribal girls her age, and her curvy hips and muscular legs suggested a more athletic role in the life of the tribespeople.

"It looks like she's already had a fair bit of practice exercising on this device," Tara said, admiring the firmness of her breasts, whose robust size was only magnified by the shadows dancing over her chest by the surrounding candles.

"I would imagine so," Gisella smiled. "I'm pretty sure each of these performers have had plenty of time to test out new techniques before going public with their first demonstration."

As the crowd applauded softly to signal their appreciation for the girl revealing herself on stage, she grabbed hold of the hanging phallus, and swung it gently between the cleft in her tits, raising her body slowly up and down on her heels while it slid between her cleavage.

"Ah," Clover nodded at the sexy display, reminding her of a stripper's routine in a gentlemen's club. "Now I'm starting to get the idea. That's a different kind of pole dance..."

"But why is the dildo *curved*?" Jessop said as his hardening pole began to bob softly between his widening legs.

"You'll see soon enough," the old lady said, angling her own legs apart as her slit began to moisten in anticipation of the native girl's erotic performance.

The girl pulled away from the articulated beam a few inches, tilting the phallus upward toward her face, then she wrapped her lips around the pole, slathering the tip of it with her circulating tongue as she pretended to give it a blowjob.

"Fuck yes," Jessop panted as his dick rose quickly between his legs. "I'd be happy to lie upside-down *too*, if I could get head like that."

"I think she's planning on giving it more than just a *blowjob*," Tara nodded, watching the girl slink down toward the base of the platform and curl her body upright in a reverse headstand.

"I figured there was some kind of gymnastics involved in this routine," Clover said. "It looks a bit like the parallel bars I played with as a kid."

The trio stared at the girl on the stage in a trance as she slowly straightened her legs above her elevated hips, then began to separate them into a perfect one-hundred-and-eighty-degree split.

"That's pretty impressive," Jessop nodded as his dick slapped against his heaving belly. "But how is she going to reach the hanging dildo in this position? It's still separated by a good foot and a half below her legs."

"Have faith, young man," Gisella smiled, peering at his impressive instrument bobbing between his legs. "Not everybody likes to have sex in the same predictable way..."

"So I'm beginning to learn," Jessop smiled as a dollop of pre-cum slipped out the slit of his crown.

Suddenly, the girl on the stage tensed her arm muscles tightly, and she began to raise her body over her planted palms toward the glistening dildo, already moistened from her earlier licking.

"Holy fuck," Tara said, watching the girl's arm and shoulder muscles flexing while she lifted her splayed pussy toward the gleaming phallus. "That's one impressive feat of athleticism–"

"Not to mention one hot-as-fuck *stripper routine*," Clover nodded.

"I'm not sure what that is, exactly," Jessop said as he grabbed hold of his throbbing hard-on and began fapping it rapidly. "But I'd sure like to be the pole right about now..."

When the girl had lifted her hips to just below the tip of the hanging phallus, she turned her splayed legs ninety degrees clockwise so they were now positioned in a cross configuration with the overhead beam, then she pressed her glistening pussy upwards a few more inches until the tip of the dildo entered her folds. The audience gasped as she grinned at them in her upside-down position, then she extended her arms all the way, driving the pole deep into her puffy folds.

"Fuck me," Clover grunted, thrusting her fingers into her own dripping pussy while she imitated the girl's fucking action of the inverted dildo. "I'm pretty sure I wouldn't have the strength to do that, but I'd sure as hell be willing to give it a try."

"I'd be happy to help," Tara chuckled, jilling her clit as she gaped at the girl on the stage, along with the rest of the mesmerized crowd. "Maybe you could crawl on my back while I supported you from below–"

"That might not be necessary after all," Clover said, watching the girl beginning to tilt her legs upward and wrap them around the perimeter of the beam while she clasped her hips tightly to the pole and circled her arms until she was hugging it with her whole body. "That looks a little more doable, if still slightly uncomfortable."

As the girl began to rock her hips gently against the swaying pole like an upside-down sloth, she began to moan softly while the three friends watched the glistening dildo disappearing in and out of her hole.

"That's pretty fucking hot," Jessop groaned as he grabbed his erection with both hands. "But I still don't understand why the dildo is curved that way?"

Gisella turned toward him, watching him stroking his darkening tool with rising excitement, and smiled.

"If you'll notice her position on the beam as the phallus it slides in and out of her pussy," she said. "You'll see that the curved end is pointed toward her belly. This provides for more direct stimulation of that part of her yoni that stimulates her juice-pouch and makes the rubbing feel that much better."

"You mean her G-spot?" Clover said, curling her own fingers upward toward the front of her dripping pussy as she felt the pressure in her pelvis beginning to build.

"Yes."

"Is that what makes her *squirt* when she climaxes?" Jessop said as copious amounts of pre-cum started to stream down the sides of his throbbing pole.

"It helps," the old lady nodded. "It stimulates the pouch to fill with more fluid so that during the final act of congress, her juices mix with her partners to facilitate the movement of his seed toward the eggs inside her belly."

"I'm pretty sure there won't be any *seeds* injected from this particular act of congress," Clover chuckled, pressing her fingers harder against the upper surface of her expanding tunnel as she felt a rising urge to pee. "But I'm sure as hell looking forward to seeing her squirt her juices all over her pretty face while she swings upside-down from that sexy apparatus."

As the girl's face began to redden and her legs started to tremble, she began to rock her body sideways on the beam, causing it to roll progressively further in swinging arcs until she suddenly swung onto the top of the pole. She quickly adjusted the position of her body, tilting it from side to side as the beam wobbled in mid-air, then when it finally came to rest, the girl held her body close to the surface of the pole before slowly resuming her humping action over the arched dildo.

But this time, with her body resting on top of the log and her parted legs revealing the entire crack of her ass, everybody could see the slippery dildo sliding in and out of her dripping folds while she hugged the round beam tightly.

"Oh my God," Tara grunted, flapping her legs together as she felt her own rising pleasure approaching like a freight train. "I have no idea how's she managing to balance that beam while she fucks the dildo, but I can't wait to see her gush all over that thing."

"I don't think it will be long now," Gisella said, reaching between Jessop's legs to caress his tightening balls while she played with her own dripping pussy. "The beam is already starting to drip from her streaming juices."

"Yes," Clover panted as she felt a river of juices pouring over her thrusting fingers. "I can feel it too–"

Suddenly, the girl on the log clenched her legs tightly around the circular beam as her body started to quiver and her thick buttock muscles began to shake, then she growled a deep groan as her juices sprayed out the back of her ass and halfway down the log. Meanwhile, the rest of the crowd groaned along in unison, squirting, jetting, and spraying their own juices over their own trembling bodies and the spectators sitting on the steps below them.

When Jessop saw the native girl shaking atop the bobbing log, Gisella squeezed his balls tightly, and he grunted in pleasure as he shot ten thick ropes of cum over her quivering thighs. Tara clamped her thighs closed while she tipped over the edge next to him, rocking her body back and forth while she groaned in simultaneous ecstasy. Clover was the last of the group to come, but when she did, she sprayed the hardest stream outward from her splayed legs, gushing her juices like a garden hose toward the edge of the stage. By the time everybody finished shaking and dripping in excitement, they peered at each other with satisfied grins.

"That's *one* way to play with a dildo," Tara panted, nodding at her blushing friends.

"And one way to squirt like a fire hose," Clover shuddered, pulling her dripping fingers out of her vulva slowly.

"I haven't cum that hard in a while," Jessop nodded, smiling at Gisella to thank her for aiding his own self-pleasure.

"Are you getting some new ideas for raising your game?" she said as she rubbed her slippery thighs together after her own powerful climax.

"A few," Jessop grinned. "I'm looking forward to seeing what the next performer does at tomorrow's performance. I'm getting just as many good ideas from the boys as the girls."

"Good," Gisella said. "Because I've slotted Tara in for the one two days from now. I hope you've all been working on your routines to impress our judges."

"Oh, we've been working on them alright," Clover nodded, staring at Jessop's flagging erection. "We've been experimenting with our *own* slightly curved dildo every chance we can get..."

9

———————

After the sexy performance of the athletic tribal girl on the elevated beam, the three friends returned to their cabin and fell asleep quickly. For almost two weeks, they'd enjoyed an erotic display on the village stage, having enjoyed at least one orgasm between them virtually every day. They needed some time to rest and replenish their sexual energy, and they slept until noon the following day.

When they woke up and headed to the square for the communal lunch, they sat next to some of the young tribespeople who'd already performed on the stage, asking how they'd come up with their new techniques for self-stimulation and looking for ideas for making their own presentations more stimulating. Clover and Jessop seemed particularly interested in learning how to make rubber molds like the one the gay youth had demonstrated, and he eagerly loaned them his device for their own practice.

Later that day, after the trio each had their turn using the device, they returned to the big amphitheater, more charged up than ever.

"It's another *boy* demonstrating tonight?" Clover said when she and the others joined Gisella near the front of the stage as the sun set over the mountains and dusk began to settle over the village square.

"Yes," Gisella nodded, happy to see their naked bodies already glistening and swelling in anticipation of another erotic performance.

"I can't wait to see what contraption they come up with *next*," Tara said, peering at the empty stage as the drumbeat announced the arrival of another presenter to the stage.

"Maybe he'll do it the old-fashioned way," Jessop chuckled. "Sometimes you don't need anything other than your own hands and a fair amount of lube for a proper wank."

"Sometimes," the old lady smiled. "But it seems our young people are always trying to stretch the envelope to impress the judges. They only get one crack at the can having a couple's hookup in front of the whole crowd."

"Are they allowed to mingle with the *rest* of the group after their initial solo performance?" Clover asked. "I imagine they must have a lot of bottled-up sexual energy to release after waiting eighteen years to show their stuff."

"Of course," Gisella laughed. "We encourage as much mingling as possible between our tribal members in order to stretch their boundaries. Everyone is eager to try out the new techniques for themselves, with or without the help of partners."

"What about *us*?" Tara said, raising an eyebrow toward the old lady. "Are we bound by the same rules as the rest of the young people? I mean, are we allowed to mingle and hookup with some of the natives before our own presentations?"

"I suppose there's nothing stopping you from doing so, since you're still considered outsiders. But if you wait to reveal your own special talents for the entire group, it will be all the more exciting for the rest of the tribe."

"Do you hear that, Jessop?" Clover said, turning to smile at her friend. "It looks like you're the only one of us to have free rein to explore the possibilities before the winners are chosen at the end of the month."

"It's crossed my mind a few times already, believe me," Jessop grinned.

"Oh?" Gisella said. "Are you more interested in pairing up with a *boy* or a *girl*?"

"I've always preferred girls," Jessop said as his tool started to twitch when he noticed another performer moving toward the stage behind the flickering candles. "But I'm not opposed to hooking up with another male if the circumstances are right..."

"Well, this one looks right up your alley," Tara chuckled, watching the youth ascend the steps at the rear of the stage and walk up to the front of the lectern with his hands clasped gently behind his back. "Young, pretty, and slightly *petite*. He might be a little more entertaining for your practice than an inanimate fuck-toy."

While the audience applauded the newcomer politely, the three friends ran their eyes over his body, admiring his lean figure and soft, brown eyes.

"He seems pretty relaxed, so far," Tara said, noticing his penis resting softly against his thighs while he peered out into the audience.

"He might be a bit shy this first time," Gisella nodded. "Sometimes it can take them a few minutes to get in the right frame of mind–"

"What is he holding behind his back?" Clover said, pinching the top of her thighs together in anticipation of yet another surprise.

Suddenly, the boy pulled a clear glass bottle from the side of his buttocks and held it up for the crowd to see. Then he slipped the long neck of the bottle between his thighs, sliding it sensuously over his tightening balls and his slowly hardening instrument.

"That's an unusual choice for a prop," Tara said, squinting her eyes at the transparent bottle. "I'm not quite sure how he's planning to use that to enhance his sexual stimulation..."

"Yes," Jessop said, spreading his legs apart and watching his own dick beginning to rise over his stomach. "He seems more interested in stimulating his *butthole* than his willie."

"He's not quite as big as some of the others," Clover nodded, feeling her pussy moistening as she watched the youth caress the underside of his perineum with the long neck of the bottle. "Maybe he's going to use the pointed end in another way–"

As if on cue, the boy tilted the neck of the bottle upwards, rolling it gently over his lengthening shaft until his erection was pointed straight up. Then he placed the lip of the bottle over his swelling glans and pushed it gently downward until his tool was halfway inside.

"Simple, but effective," Jessop grunted, grabbing hold of his hard-on and stroking it in unison with the blushing youth.

"It's actually kind of *hot*," Tara shuddered, circling her clit while she stared at the cute boy. "There's something about seeing his pink dick poking inside the transparent bottle..."

"Yes," Clover huffed as she slid her fingers inside her throbbing tunnel. "At least we can see all of his body this time. There's nothing blocking our view."

"He seems to be getting more excited now," Jessop

nodded, noticing the boy's glans turning a darker shade of red as he thrust his dick deeper into the neck of the flask.

"Yes," Clover said, noticing the boy tensing his muscles as he pulled the bottle harder over his swelling instrument.

Suddenly, the boy's expression changed as his forehead wrinkled while he peered down at the bottle, grasping it with two hands while he tried to move it over his shaft.

"What's going on?" Tara said, leaning forward as she squinted at the boy's locked hips. "It almost looks like his cock is *stuck* in the bottle."

"I think it *is*," Clover nodded, pulling her fingers out of her pussy while she peered at him with a furrowed brow.

"Talk about being bottled up!" Jessop chuckled as he paused his own stroking.

"What are we going to do?" Clover said, becoming increasingly concerned while she stared at the panicked look on the boy's face.

"Can't he use some *lube* to reduce the friction inside the bottle?" Tara said.

"I think it's too late for that," Gisella said. "It looks like he's got his erection inserted all the way inside and he can't pull it out."

"Can't we just *break* the bottle to free it?" Clover said, noticing the tip of his hard-on starting to turn purple. "It looks like his blood flow is being restricted, and his cock is just swelling larger–"

"That would risk cutting his penis and disfiguring him forever," the old lady said, lifting her hands over her knees while trying to figure out what to do. "It might even cause a gash that couldn't be closed, causing him to bleed out."

"There's got to be *something* we can do!" Clover said, feeling more and more worried about the frightened youth's predicament as he yanked on the bottle more desperately.

"His penis will be damaged either way if his blood flow isn't restored fairly soon."

"As long as his penis remains swollen and erect, I don't see what else we can do," Gisella said as the rest of the crowd began to stand up, murmuring amongst themselves about how they could assist the helpless youth.

"I've got an idea," Clover said, suddenly jumping to her feet. "Tara, go get some aloe vera from the forest while go to the boy's aid. Then join me on the stage when you return. Go quickly!"

Tara leaped off her step and rushed into the forest behind their cabin, where they'd found the aloe plants growing the previous day. Then Jessop peered at Clover with a curious expression.

"What are you going to do?" he said. "Gisella said that extra lube wasn't likely to help the situation–"

"Something that worked earlier with *you*," Clover smiled, rolling the tip of her tongue over her upper lip. "Watch and learn, my young friend."

Clover rushed toward the front of the stage, then she leaped up onto the platform, pulling the boy down onto his knees.

"Help me, please," the boy pleaded as he gazed at Clover with a terrified expression.

"We're going to fix this," she nodded, pressing him gently onto his back and pushing his knees forward, toward his chest.

When Tara returned to the stadium, she joined Clover on the stage, holding two shoots of aloe leaves up in the air with their tips removed.

"What do you want me to do with these?" she said, glancing at Clover with wide eyes.

"First, I want you to hold his legs while you bend him

backward," Clover said. "We need to get his circulation moving out of his lower body. I'm going to stimulate him over his perineum while you slather the base of his cock with the lube. If we can somehow get him to climax, his erection should begin to shrink, allowing it to slide out of the bottle..."

"How exactly are you planning to make him come?" Tara said, squinting at her friend in confusion. "That's the *last* thing he seems to be interested in doing at this precise moment–"

"Trust me," Clover said, lowering her head toward the boy's shaking midsection. "Just get ready to pull on the bottle when I give you the signal."

"Okay," Tara said, shaking her head in dismay.

Clover grabbed one of the aloe leaves from her hand and squirted a heavy drop of cream over the boy's tight balls, then she cupped her hands over his sac, caressing his testicles as he started to moan.

"Does that feel good?" she said, peering at the boy's frightened face.

He nodded silently, then he peered up at Tara, whose tits were dangling over his face while she pulled his legs over his shoulders.

"That's it, Tara," Clover nodded, lowering her face closer toward the boy's rising ass while she stretched out her tongue toward his puckering sphincter.

"Here goes nothing," she panted. "Let's hope this puts him over the edge..."

When she placed her mouth over his tingling rosebud, the boy groaned loudly, tilting his hips further upward while he eagerly pressed his butt harder toward Clover's face. As she circled her tongue over his starfish and ran rapid figure-eight patterns like she did when she was licking

Tara's clit, the boy began to hump his hips upward, making the bottle flap wildly in the air.

"Put some lube over the base of his dick," Clover said to Tara, lifting her head temporarily. "Then hold the bottle while he rocks it and I lick his butthole."

"Okay," Tara said, pressing her shoulders down over the back of the boy's feet as she lowered her tits onto his face while she squirted some aloe over his bouncing mound and clasped the sides of the bottle tightly.

As the boy's pleasure began to steadily rise while he planted his face between Tara's rocking breasts and Clover stimulated his anus with her tongue and his tightening balls with her hands, he arched his hips higher in the air, grunting ever louder. Suddenly, he jerked his hips harder over his shaking body, and the two girls saw thick streams of creamy fluid jetting into the hollow cavity of the bottle.

"You did it!" Tara shouted, watching the boy ejaculate into the bottle.

"Okay," Clover said, pulling her body away from the boy's pulsating perineum while he finished coming into the container. "Now relax his legs and pull yourself away from his body. The less sexual stimulation he has right now, the better. We need his dick to detumesce as quickly as possible. If you see his erection beginning to shrink, squirt some more lube over the lip of the bottle and try to pull his penis out."

After a few seconds, the two girls noticed the boy's erection starting to lighten in color as his circulation returned to normal, then his glans started to shrivel as his hard-on tilted toward the bottom of the bottle.

"Try it now," Clover nodded toward Tara. "It should be easier to pull his penis out now."

Tara tugged on the bottle softly, and a few seconds later,

the boy's shriveling pole popped out the end of the flask, dropping loudly onto his slippery stomach. He reached down with his two hands to make sure he could still feel sensation in his member, then he peered up at Clover, smiling softly.

"All better?" she said, raising her eyebrows hopefully.

"Yes," he said, nodding up toward Tara, who simultaneously relaxed her grip on his legs. "Thank you both for helping me."

"Our pleasure," Tara said. "We were just glad we could help."

"No," the boy grinned, staring up at Tara's bobbing tits and her elf ears poking out the sides of her pink hair. "The pleasure was all mine."

As everyone in the stands rose to their feet and applauded the performance of the two visitors to the stage, Gisella turned toward Jessop and nodded softly.

"It looks like your friends got to demonstrate their skills a little earlier than planned on our stage tonight."

"You haven't seen anything, yet," Jessop grinned. "Just wait until you see what Tara's got planned for tomorrow night."

"I can hardly wait," the old lady said, feeling her pussy tingling at the thought of seeing the sexy elf show off her body for everyone to enjoy.

10

———

After the scary performance with the boy and the bottle, the three friends returned to their cabin, feeling their hearts pounding in their chests.

"That was crazy," Jessop said, peering at Clover with wide eyes. "How did you know that licking his *asshole* would free his dick?"

"I wasn't entirely sure," Clover said. "But when I saw how fast and how hard you came when I did the same to you a few days ago, I figured it was our best chance to reduce the swelling."

"It sure worked pretty fast," Tara nodded. "He almost filled that *entire* bottle with his cum when he climaxed."

"I think you might have helped a little," Clover chuckled. "While shaking your tits over his face as you pulled his legs over his shoulders."

"That was pretty hot, actually," Tara said. "The poor boy probably never knew what hit him when you started probing his pucker."

"I'm just glad it was a happy ending, if you know what I mean," Clover said.

"Yes," Tara laughed. "In more ways than one."

"Speaking of *happy endings*," Jessop said, winking at Tara. "Are you ready for tomorrow night's performance?"

"Well, I've certainly been practicing enough," Tara smiled. "I think I've perfected the self-sucking technique. Now it's just a question of how much of a surprise it will be for the rest of the tribespeople. I'm not sure it will be special enough to impress the judges."

"I don't think you have to worry about that," Clover grinned, swiping her palm over Tara's upturned breasts. "With that figure and your flexibility, I'm sure you'll have them eating out of your hands in no time."

The following day, the trio made their way back to the amphitheater, with Tara holding back in the shadows behind the stage while the candles were illuminated and the drummer announced the introduction of the next performer. After the sun had set behind the mountains, Tara walked unsteadily up the stairs at the back of the platform, feeling her legs shaking while the audience clapped politely at the appearance of another newcomer. When she reached the center of the dais, she paused with her hands resting over her bare mound, feeling her nipples tingling in the cool evening air. She had shaved her mound and her vulva with a little help from Clover, so the crowd would be able to better watch her lick her pussy, and suddenly she felt exposed and vulnerable on the stage.

"She seems a little nervous," Jessop said, glancing at his trembling friend on the stage.

"She just needs to get in the rhythm," Clover said, nodding toward Tara confidently. "Once she gets started and begins to feel the pleasure from her self-stimulation, she'll soon forget that everybody is watching her."

"No props today?" Gisella said, sitting between the two of them on the front steps of the theater.

"There's no need," Clover nodded, feeling her pussy throbbing at the thought of watching her friend licking herself in full view of the entire crowd. "She's going to be doing something I suspect none of your people have seen before."

"Well, you've certainly got my interest now," the old lady said, rubbing the sides of her thighs against Jessop's and Clover's soft skin.

When the crowd's applause receded, Tara nodded in acknowledgement, then she lowered herself onto the soft rugs lining the surface of the stage and lay down on her back with her legs extended straight out in front of her. Then she bent her knees and raised her legs over her shoulders, slowly straightening them until her feet rested on the dais behind her head.

"That's some pretty impressive flexibility," Gisella nodded, parting her own legs as she stared at Tara's exposed, bare pussy.

"She's just getting started," Clover said. "You haven't seen anything yet."

Tara placed both of her hands behind her knees, then she lifted her face a few inches, threading her feet behind her head in a crossed-over position. This had the effect of curling her body further into a forward arch position, with her buttock cheeks pulled apart so the crowd could clearly see her pink rosebud and glistening vulva gleaming next to the flickering candles.

"That's quite a specimen," Gisella nodded as she drifted

her hand over her mound while two dribbles of liquid dripped out of her pussy.

"You have no idea," Clover grinned, happy to see the old lady enjoying herself so early in the presentation. "Tara is full of surprises."

While Tara flexed her legs a bit harder, her spine curled a few degrees further, moving her face closer to her steaming snatch. A murmur rose from the audience as they looked at one another in surprise, wondering what the sexy elf was going to do next. But when they saw her long tongue snake out of her mouth and slide over her pearl, a collective gasp emanated from the grandstand.

"You weren't kidding," Gisella grunted, curling her own abdomen as she rubbed her fingers over her dripping slit. "I see that your friend has *multiple* talents."

"It doesn't hurt that she has a longer appendage than the rest of us," Clover nodded, feeling her own pussy throbbing while she watched Tara slide her tongue down her gleaming slit.

"Even her *bean* looks bigger than most girls," Gisella panted, pinching her clit between her fingers and rubbing it softly.

"It might have something to do with her rising level of pleasure from displaying herself for the viewing pleasure of the tribe," Clover said. "I haven't seen her pussy swollen to this degree in a long time."

The old lady nodded with her mouth agape while she stared at Tara sucking her own clit.

"I have a suspicion there's a few hundred *other* eager mouths ready to suck on that pretty jewel right about now."

"So it would seem," Clover chuckled, peering around the amphitheater, noticing many of the tribespeople had their mouths wide open while their tongues absentmindedly mimicked Tara's licking technique.

As Tara started to groan in rising pleasure from her self-stimulation, her curled body began to rock back and forth on the soft animal skins, alternately highlighting her tight rosebud and her dripping labia in the surrounding candlelight. But when she crunched her body even further and flicked the tip of her tongue over her tingling sphincter, the crowd with her, jerking and jilling themselves shamelessly as they watched the sexy elf quivering and shaking in her hunched-over position. It was obvious to everybody that Tara was rapidly approaching the point of no return as her arms trembled holding her tensing thighs, and when she lowered her head directly over her flaring bulb and began sucking it harder, a torrent of juices began pouring out of her slit and down the crack of her ass.

As her face progressively darkened to a deep shade of red, she gripped her legs as tightly as she could, tensing her entire body in preparation for the biggest orgasm of her life. When she felt the wave of pleasure finally burst, a huge spray of juices suddenly jetted straight up in the air out of her pulsing pussy, drenching the back of her head and her soaking face while she blinked her eyelashes and felt her clit throbbing in her mouth. As she squirted one long spray after another like a geyser, her pucker flexed and contracted in powerful spasms, causing the rest of the crowd to moan and squirt along with her, drenching all the other naked spectators sitting on the lower steps.

"Holy *fuckkkk*," Jessop groaned, shooting one long rope of cum after another between his legs without even touching himself.

"I've never seen her come like that," Clover grunted

while gripping the insides of her thighs as she sprayed her own juices over Gisella's quivering legs.

"I'm not sure *I* have either," the old lady panted, jerking her body up and down in simultaneous pleasure. "That might have been the sexiest thing I've ever seen."

"Does that mean Tara's in the running to win a spot in the couple's presentation later this month?" Clover asked.

"Without a doubt," Gisella nodded, wiping her dripping hands over the edges of her thighs. "There are still a few more performers to go before the full moon, but it's hard to imagine someone topping that performance."

"You haven't seen what *Clover* can do yet," Jessop chuckled, winking at his friend while she held a finger to her lips. "Tara's not the *only* one harboring a little surprise..."

~

R eady for more erotic chills and thrills? Read the next volume in Clover's Fantasy Adventures: Coming of Age, Part 3. Buy direct and save at victoriarusherotica. Or download from your favorite online bookstore here: retailer links.

In the remote village of Whisperwood, there are a thousand ways to pleasure yourself...

ALSO BY VICTORIA RUSH

Adult Fairytales:

The Enchanted Forest: An Erotic Fairytale

The Land of Giants: An Erotic Fairytale

The Dragon's Lair: An Erotic Fairytale

Witch's Brew: An Erotic Fairytale

The Mage's Spell: An Erotic Fairytale

The Mermaid Lagoon: An Erotic Fairytale

The Coven: An Erotic Fairytale

Rapunzel: An Erotic Fairytale

The Seven Dwarfs: An Erotic Fairytale

The Land of Mutants: An Erotic Fairytale

The Erotic Temple: A Sexy Fairytale (Coming Soon)

Erotica Themed Bundles:

Voyeur: Lesbian Erotica Bundle

Public Affairs: A Lesbian Anthology

Futa Fantasies: The Ladyboy Collection

Threesomes: The Lesbian Collection

Threesomes - Volume 2: The Lesbian Collection

First Time: A Lesbian Anthology

Hedonism: An Erotic Anthology

Switch Hitters: Bisexual Erotica

Taboo Erotica: The Lesbian Series

BDSM: The Lesbian Collection

Party Games: The Erotic Collection

Party Games 2: The Erotic Collection

All Girl 1: Lesbian Erotica Bundle

All Girl 2: Lesbian Erotica Bundle

All Girl 3: Lesbian Erotica Bundle

All Girl 4: Lesbian Erotica Bundle

Erotic Fairytale Bundles:

Clover's Fantasy Adventures: Books 1 - 5

Clover's Fantasy Adventures: Books 6 - 10

Erotic Fantasy:

Pirate's Bounty: A Time Travel Adventure

Wild West: A Time Travel Adventure

Private Riley: A Time Travel Adventure

Cleopatra's Secret: A Time Travel Adventure

Bounty Hunter 2125: A Time Travel Adventure

Ninja Assassin: A Time Travel Adventure

The 300: A Time Travel Adventure

Arabian Nights: An Erotic Fairytale (coming soon...)

Steamy Time Travel Bundles:

Riley's Time Travel Adventures: Books 1 - 5

Lesbian Erotica:

The Dinner Party: Lesbian Voyeur Erotica

The Darkroom: Bisexual Voyeur Erotica

Naked Yoga: Lesbian Transgender Erotica

Nude Cruise: Bisexual Voyeur Erotica

Rush Hour: Taboo Public Sex

The Girl Next Door: First Time Lesbian Erotic Romance

Girls' Camp: Lesbian Group Sex

Wet Dream: Ladyboy Fantasy Erotica

The Convent: Taboo Sex with a Nun

Sex Robot: A Dream Sex Machine

The Personal Trainer: Getting Pumped at the Gym

The Dominatrix: BDSM Lesbian Domination

Webcam Chat: Lesbian Online Sex

Paint Me: A Kinky Bodypainting Workshop

The Toy Party: Girls Sharing Sex Toys

The Costume Party: Strapping One On

Swedish Sauna: Lesbian Group Sex

The Therapist: Taboo Lesbian Erotica

Elevator Shaft: Bisexual Threesomes Erotica

Ladyboy: Lesbian Transgender Erotica

Peep Show: Lesbian Voyeur Erotica

The Dare: Public Sex Erotica

Maid Service: Lesbian Threesomes Erotica

The Hitchhiker: First Time Lesbian Erotica

The Housesitter: Spycam Lesbian Erotica

The Spa: Lesbian Group Orgy

Parlor Games: Blindfold Sex Party

The Exchange Student: First Time Lesbian Erotica

The Hostel: Bisexual Group Erotica

The Harem: Lesbian Erotic Romance

The Orient Express: Lesbian Voyeur Erotica

The First Lady: A Forbidden Lesbian Erotic Romance

The Slave: Lesbian BDSM Erotica

The Masseuse: Lesbian Sensuous Erotica

Too Close for Comfort: Lesbian Forbidden Erotica

Naked Twister: A Wild Party Game

Lexi: The Sex App (Lesbian Fantasy Erotica)

Call Girl: Lesbian Bisexual Threesomes Erotica

Circle Jill: Lesbian Masturbation Workshop

The Viewing Room: Masturbation Voyeur Erotica

Spin the Bottle: A Kinky Party Game

The Hair Salon: Lesbian Voyeur Erotica

Tribadism 1: Girls Only Sex Workshop

Tribadism 2: The Art of Scissoring

Tribadism 3: Threeway Hookups

The Kiss: A Game of Oral Sex

Pledge Week: Sorority Sisters

Carny Games 1: A Wild Sex Party

Carny Games 2: A Kinky Sex Party

Carny Games 3: An Erotic Sex Party

Dreamscape: An Artificial Reality Game

Glory Hole: Guess Who's On the Other Side

Joy Ride: A Late Night Erotic Bus Trip

The Blind Girl: An Erotic Romance(Coming Soon)

Lesbian Erotica Bundles:

Jade's Erotic Adventures: Books 1 - 5

Jade's Erotic Adventures: Books 6 - 10

Jade's Erotic Adventures: Books 11 - 15

Jade's Erotic Adventures: Books 16 - 20

Jade's Erotic Adventures: Books 21 - 25

Jade's Erotic Adventures: Books 26 - 30

Jade's Erotic Adventures: Books 31 - 35

Jade's Erotic Adventures: Books 36 - 40

Jade's Erotic Adventures: Books 41 - 45

Jade's Erotic Adventures: Books 46 - 50

Fifty Shades of Jade: Superbundle

Standalone Stories:

The Polynesian Girl: A Lesbian EroticRomance